"Her eyes were just above the level of the water. The surface was raked by a light breeze. The bay stretched out toward the sea. The distant pine-covered islands were misted over, but the water close by flashed in the sun. The only sounds, above the sound of the water, were those of the dog sloshing through the mud, the rustle of the grass as it gave way for the passage of his body.

"The girl lay in the sun awhile, rolled over and stood up. She studied the sailboat, then the water. She turned and plunged into the bay. . . ."

A Quiet Place is the story of a girl's first awareness of herself as an adult and a woman, her weakness for one boy and her friendship with another, less sophisticated boy, who falls in love with her.

The story evokes the simple pleasures found in a quiet place in Maine, the pleasures and pain of approaching maturity, for the girl, for a boy who has spent his life on a farm, and for a disillusioned boy who thinks of himself as a man of the world.

A QUIET PLACE

by Peter Burchard

tempo books

GROSSET & DUNLAP, INC.
A National General Company
Publishers   New York

Copyright © 1972 by Peter Burchard
All rights reserved

Tempo Books Edition 1974
Reprinted by arrangement with
Coward, McCann & Geoghegan

Tempo Books is registered in the
U.S. Patent Office

ISBN: 0-448-05722-0

Published simultaneously in Canada

Printed in the United States of America

For Lee

A QUIET PLACE

1

The girl struck out across the sunny fields, walking toward the bay. She wore a bright bikini. Her skin was tan. Her blond hair had a faintly reddish cast.

A small hound, brown and white, ran after the girl, catching up to her near a stand of white birch, wagging and jumping. She knelt in the path, patting the dog, letting him nuzzle one of her ears. As she started down the hill again, the dog ran ahead, dashing into the tall grass.

A meadowlark flew up from her nest. The girl called the dog, throwing a stick to divert his attention.

A Quiet Place

The tide was in, the marsh grass awash. A great yellow rock served as the jumping-off point for a pier whose timbers had been bleached by salt and sun. At the end of the pier, tied to a float, a sailboat bobbed gently on the water. The girl walked down the short gangplank connecting the float to the end of the pier. She spread out her towel and lay down, facing the sun.

Her eyes were just above the level of the water. The surface was raked by a light breeze. The bay stretched out toward the sea. The distant, pine-covered islands were misted over, but the water close by flashed in the sun. The only sounds, above the sound of the water, were those of the dog sloshing through the mud, the rustle of the grass as it gave way for the passage of his body.

The girl lay in the sun awhile, rolled over and stood up. She studied the sailboat, then the water. She turned and plunged into the bay, swam halfway to a small island, a hundred yards or so offshore, turned and swam back to the float, her arms gleaming. As she did so, the dog, whose tail was moving constantly, leaving no doubt about where he was, ran along the shore, leaped to the pier, and

A Quiet Place

came out to greet the girl. His legs were black with mud. The girl said softly, "You've done it again."

She lay on her stomach. The dog lay close to her, his chin resting on his paws.

The dog growled, low in his throat. He ran along the pier, back to shore, barking as he went. The girl stood up, facing some trees just beyond the rock.

Three boys walked down the slope and mounted the rock. One of them came ahead of the others. He was handsome, his hair dark, his skin deeply tanned. He was wearing a pair of narrow-waisted jeans.

The girl adjusted her bikini top. She greeted the dark boy. "Hi, Mark."

"Hello, Cindy." He moved along the pier with studied ease. Halfway down the gangplank, he sat sat down, forcing the others to sit on the pier. He motioned toward the older of the boys on the pier. "This is a friend of mine, David Roth. Guess you know my brother, Sam."

David Roth was thin and shy. Looking toward the little island, he said earnestly, "It's beautiful here."

Mark clasped his hands around his knees. "And quiet," he said.

Cindy said, "Too quiet."

A Quiet Place

Sam was younger than the other boys. Cindy greeted him. "Why aren't you working today, Sam?"

"I start at one."

Mark took off his sandals, tossed them over the rock, and half turned to the boys behind him. "Don't let that dog run away with my sandals." He looked openly at the girl, up and down.

She said, cooly, "My dog's name is Brindle."

She worked the towel across her back, drying herself against a freshening breeze, draped it around her shoulders, holding the corners together in front.

Mark spoke again, in a gentler tone. "We came to ask you to come to a picnic."

"I'm going to the Thornes' for supper tonight."

"We thought we'd have a picnic tomorrow night."

"I'd like to come tomorrow."

"Who are the Thornes?"

"My father made friends with Ike Thorne last year. He invited us to visit their farm. This year I'm learning how to milk."

"Is Ike the hayseed that delivers eggs?"

Cindy's eyes flashed. She said, "Ike Thorne is a friend of mine."

A Quiet Place

Mark stood up and moved aside. He said, "I didn't know he was a special friend."

Sam said, "I hope you'll come tomorrow night."

Cindy smiled. "Of course I'll come."

The girl and the three boys drifted up the hill, talking and laughing. Mark ran ahead with the dog at his heels. He found an old tennis ball in the path and threw it, watching as the dog ran after it.

The house was a bungalow, white with a granite step at the back door. Beside the door, tilting on a slight rise, was a shabby jeep.

The dog, nose down, moved toward the road. The girl called him anxiously. Mark and David walked ahead, going toward the jeep. Cindy said, " 'Bye, Sam."

"See you tomorrow."

Mark gunned the jeep's engine. Sam broke away and jumped in beside the driver. All four wheels bit the earth, kicking up dust.

Cindy turned and went inside. She called, "Dad?"

There was no answer. She threw the towel over the back of a chair and changed into jeans and a faded blue shirt. She went out a side door, dropping her bathing suit on the ground. The grass around

A Quiet Place

the house had just been cut. Beyond the short grass was a thick fringe of juniper and, beyond that, still taller grass where an old hayrick, long since abandoned, leaned against the brightness of the bay and the distant profile of Bass Island. She walked into the taller grass, picked a small bunch of purple vetch and turned back to the house, adding a buttercup as she went. She found an empty jelly glass, filled it with water and arranged the bouquet, putting the buttercup in the middle. She stood a moment at the door of her room, holding the flowers, then turned back and put them on a table which was covered with letters and unpaid bills.

The dog whimpered, scratching at the screen.

"Stay, Brindle," Cindy said. "You have to stay here."

She hung her bathing suit on the line with her father's swimming trunks and one of his yellowed tennis shirts. She went out the driveway to the mailbox. The little metal flag was down. She pulled the mailbox door open, fished the mail out, looked through it, and put it back. She glanced at her watch and started walking.

As she approached a fork in the road, a place where three houses stood in a cluster, she heard the

A Quiet Place

sounds of tennis and men's voices. The court was screened from the road by a row of tall trees growing along a stone wall and smaller trees, thick spruce, between the others. She stood in the road, listening. The men finished a game and started switching courts. The girl called, "Dad?"

Her father came and looked out between the trees. He said, "How long have you been there, Cindy girl?"

"A minute or two. I'm going to the Thornes. They invited me for supper."

"Yes, I remember."

"See you later."

2

Cindy turned into the front yard. Astride the ridgepole of the barn stood a cupola, newer than the rest of the building, crowned by a weather vane, its golden horse racing with the wind. She looked toward the house and turned toward the barn, stopping by a fence to watch some sheep where they'd gathered in a pasture littered with stones. Beyond the sheep, set against the shadow of the trees beyond, was an old car, a Model T the color of rust, poised where its engine had coughed its last, waiting for a decent burial.

The barn loomed against the sky, a huge frame structure with naked shiplap siding, gray from salt

A Quiet Place

and driving rain. Beside the door lay an old harrow, its whales' teeth resting on the hard-packed soil, and, beyond it, on a battered cradle, rested an old wooden boat, its rib showing in a number of places. One of the barn doors stood wide open. One was shut. On the one that was shut was a bent and rusting metal sign. NO SMOKING.

Sunlight warmed a wedge of barn floor, touching one end of a heavy yoke where it lay against the wall of an enclosed stall. The girl stepped into the barn, calling without expecting any answer. "Ike. You here?"

The hayloft was all but empty now. Wisps of hay trailed from its edge. Sunlight filtered through a lone window. The spider webs shone like white gold. A swallow streaked by the girl's head, flying a certain course, ending on a beam where she'd built her nest.

The girl went through a short corridor and entered the tie room, where the cows were milked. The stalls were empty. On one side, a small stall housed a month-old calf, a golden beast with liquid eyes. The stalls along the wall were empty. The girl

A Quiet Place

peered into the barnyard, looking through one of the sliding windows. The cows were standing patiently on a slope near the corner of the yard. The oxen were sunning out by the gate, looking stupidly toward the house.

The girl slid the door open, moving it a foot or so. She leaned out. Some of the cows came toward the door. She shut it again.

The girl turned to the calf who was standing watching her intently. The beast nudged her pail with the nipple at the bottom. "You have to wait," the girl said.

The floor was clean, except in the far corner. The girl took up a shovel and tidied the corner, slid one of the windows open, and tossed the cow dung into the yard. She scooped a shovelful of sawdust out of a barrel and spread it around behind the stalls. She went back out to the front yard.

The house, once white, had grown gray. The shutters were a pale green, the paint flaking. The porch sagged pleasantly. Its railing was missing several vertical members. Three old rockers faced the yard.

As the girl approached the house, a small white

A Quiet Place

dog, old and rickety, roused herself, her tail signaling a greeting.

A truck stacked with bales of hay turned into the yard. Two men were in its cab. When he saw the girl, the driver shouted and banged the truck door with his fist. He jumped down, grinning, motioning toward the man who was with him. "You never meet Henry? This is Henry."

Henry hopped down, smiling toothlessly. The other man, tall and lean, gestured toward the bay where it winked between the dark pines. He looked down, nudging Henry. "Henry and I are hayin' partners. We just baled enough hay to fill a dozen barns."

Henry smiled again. He said, "Ike here. He's the champ. 'Course I'm three times as old as him."

Ike said, "Cindy, you seen my parents?"

She shook her head.

"What day is it today? I been goin' so strong I don't know what day of the week it is."

"Friday," the girl said.

"Mother takes Father to the doctor Fridays."

Henry said, "How's your father comin'?"

"Father's gainin'," Ike said. He turned to the girl.

A Quiet Place

"Henry and I got to unload the truck." He grinned again, his teeth white in his tan face. "How'd you like to fill the troughs with water? And you can do some sweeping if you like. And spread sawdust behind the stalls. By the time you finish we'll be ready to milk."

"I already did the floor."

One of Ike's sinewy arms shot out. He rested a hand on Cindy's shoulder. He bunched his other hand into a fist and menaced her nose. He said, "Cindy's my helper. She's company." He moved toward the truck.

Henry asked, "Is she a good milker?"

"Cindy's gainin'," Ike said.

She went back to the tie room, took a bucket off its nail, filled the troughs, carrying the bucket back and forth to a faucet in a corner, sat on a milking stool, and leaned against the wall.

Ike poked his head into the room. "We've finished," he said. "I better drive Henry home. His wife will howl if he comes home late."

"I'd just as soon walk it," Henry called. "It's only five minutes through the woods."

"All right, Henry," Ike said. "You got somethin' comin'. We won't forget."

A Quiet Place

"Never mind," Henry said. "Some o' your mother's cheese'll suit us."

"There you go gittin' greedy. Mother's the one to decide what suits you."

He flung the tie room door open, bellowing the cows' names. Four out of five hobbled over the sill, leaving the oxen and a brown and white cow. Ike shouted, "Come along. What's the matter with you there, Clover?"

"Cindy, go out and give Clover a whack. After she calved, she wouldn't go out. Now she won't come in. Critter doesn't know what she wants."

After supper, just before dark, Ike drove her home. He stopped the truck near the mailbox. The engine idled rhythmically. He said, "You'll be back tomorrow, won't you, Cindy?"

"I'd love to, Ike, but I can't tomorrow."

"Sunday maybe."

"Maybe Sunday.'

"Come to dinner. My mother's parents come to dinner Sundays. I know they want to see you before you leave." He held the wheel tightly, looking straight ahead at the deepening shadows.

"I want to see them, too."

A Quiet Place

One of his hands slid down to his knee. "Come early," he said.

She opened the door and jumped down. "I'll come as early as I can."

3

The jeep bumped in, turning sharply as it came to a stop. Mark, alone this time, sat straight up in the driver's seat. He blew the horn, a short blast, looking toward the bay.

Cindy opened her bedroom door and put her head out. "Are you busy, Dad? Can you ask him in?"

Her father said, "I never answer to horns."

"Hush, Dad. He'll hear you." She went to the window and called, "Mark, come in and meet my father. I'll be ready in a few minutes."

She watched while he jumped down from the

A Quiet Place

jeep, then went back to drying her hair, rubbing it with a fresh towel.

She heard her father say, "Hello. You must be Mark."

"Yes, sir."

"Sit down. Cindy won't be long."

"Beautiful view you have here."

"It's peaceful here. Fine for me but not the best place in the world for Cindy. I'm glad she met some people in the village."

"And the Thornes. I understand she knows the Thornes."

Cindy combed her hair. It lay wet against her head. She put on a clean shirt, her patched jeans and heavy leather sandals. She reached for a circular pair of earrings and hooked them through her pierced lobes. She rubbed her cheeks.

As she opened the door, she said, "Hello, Mark."

"Hi."

Mark stood up, facing Cindy's father. "My mother said Cindy can stay if she wants to. She can spend the night instead of coming back."

Her father said, "Thanks. I'll call your mother."

Cindy and Mark climbed into the jeep. Mark swung it in a wide arc, running through the tall

A Quiet Place

grass. She said, "Stop at the mailbox a minute, will you?"

The jeep stopped, engine throbbing, while Cindy jumped down and put a postcard in the box. She raised the little metal flag. "Thanks," she said. "Getting a card off to my mother."

"You live mostly with your father?"

"When I'm not in school. My mother's out in Colorado."

The jeep jumped forward to the blacktop, picking up speed. There were no doors, just low metal barriers. The road became a series of horizontal blurs. She grasped the edge of her seat, looking toward the bay instead of down or dead ahead.

He gave her a quick, sidelong look. He said, "I'm not as bad a driver as that."

"It's not your driving."

"What is it then?"

"A touch of vertigo, I guess."

They stopped abruptly in front of the house, a fine old structure with a widow's walk. Sam was sitting on the grass in front. Mark called to him, "David around?"

"Upstairs. Hi, Cindy."

"Hello, Sam."

A Quiet Place

Mark said, "The food's in the kitchen. All we need is drinks." He teased Sam. "Can't send a boy to do a man's errand. I'll buy a quart of wine and a pack of Cokes."

Cindy jumped down. "I'll help Sam bring out the stuff."

Sam stood up as she moved toward him. She asked, "Who's coming?"

"Just Mark and me and David Roth and my sister. I invited Dori Carlsen. I hope her mother will let her come. By the way, your father talked to my mother. He said it's OK if you want to spend the night."

"Where does Dori live?"

"Across the street. Near the corner."

"Let's go over."

They walked to Dori's house. Sam knocked at the side door. A plump woman came out of the darkness. She had a pleasant face. Sam croaked, "Hello, Mrs. Carlsen. Is Dori in?"

"I expect her back in a few minutes."

Cindy said, "We're hoping she can come to a picnic tonight."

Dori's mother gave Cindy a long look. "I think so," she said. "If she's home by eleven."

A Quiet Place

"Fine," Sam said.

"Where are you going?"

"Out to Bass Island."

Dori's mother frowned: "I don't want Dori swimming at night."

"I won't swim either," Sam said. "It's much too chilly to swim at night."

When the jeep was loaded, Dori came out. Her sweater was the color of melted butter. Her eyes were bright. She and Sam sat in the back of the jeep. A pleasant-looking girl with straight, brown hair climbed into David's car with him. As they started off, Mark yelled at David, "Take the left fork at the end of the North Road." Then he said, under his breath, "He didn't hear me."

Cindy said, "Doesn't your sister know the way?"

"She should."

They got away fast, keeping David's car in sight, skirted the village, and stopped at a light. David, who had made the light went on ahead.

Sam and Dori talked in the back seat. Sam said something in an undertone, and Dori said, "Yes. Yes, I think so."

Cindy turned to Mark and said, "Dori's mother wants her home by eleven."

"Did you tell her we'd be back by then?"

"We promised."

"Christ. Why did you do that?"

"Because Sam wanted her to come."

"I'm sorry," Dori said. "When my father's away, my mother's strict."

"It doesn't matter," Mark said coldly.

As they crossed the causeway, the water was racing under the bridge. The sky was blood red in the west, the water shining in the distance. Mark was driving fast. As he took a curve beyond a culvert, the jeep rocked and righted itself. They tunneled through a deep pine forest on a straight stretch.

Mark said, "Let's stop at Speare's for a quart of chowder. On second thought, let's make it two."

Dori said, "Chowder really makes a picnic."

Speare's was busy. There were dozens of cars parked on the slope in front and people waiting on the lawn for tables. Mark went to the takeout window. He came back with a big paper bag, walking fast, dodging people on the grass, the lights of the restaurant at his back.

4

Speare's was an outpost. From there on, the road was lonely.

The headlights were dimmer than they should have been, marking an uncertain path. They passed a farmhouse, black against the evening sky, a yellow light burning in one of its windows. A dog barked, the sound uncertain, rising about the complaints of the engine, the whine of the heavily treaded tires.

Mark hunched above the wheel. He wiped the windshield with the heel of his hand. "Fork's someplace up ahead."

He braked and they skidded to a stop, just miss-

A Quiet Place

ing taillights dimly glowing. Mark yelled, "Christ, I almost hit you."

David said, "Ann said to go left, but I figured we better wait for you."

The jeep's wheels spun, and Mark led off.

The road ended on a bluff, widening into a parking space. Cindy jumped down. She moved up to the edge of the dunes, to a place where the blacktop crumbled. A lone car was parked on the far side of the lot, the couple in it huddled together. The beach was deserted, a sandy waste. The waves broke, hissing as they spread themselves across the flats. The tide was rising. The sea was up. In the half-light the water was dark, a void until a wave crested, crisp and white. Beyond the breakers were the shapes of rocks, black against the sea. Beyond the rocks, mists gathered, bringing the edge of the world closer.

Cindy was startled by Mark's voice behind her. "How about helping us carry the stuff?"

In the dark, Mark's face was a formless blob. Cindy turned back to the water. "I'll be with you in a minute."

They found a partly sheltered place in front of the dunes and dug a pit. Sam and Dori went off to look for wood, Dori talking excitedly. David rum-

A Quiet Place

maged in a carton, bringing out napkins and paper plates. Ann said, "We better help look for wood."

Cindy brought out a box of food. She and Mark started cutting hamburger rolls and making patties.

The others brought in armloads of wood, and they built a fire, shielding it with their bodies. As it crackled and spat, they moved back. When the flames died, they cooked their supper, their faces glowing in the orange light.

After supper, David and Ann went for a walk. Sam and Dori wandered off, holding hands.

Mark said, "That kid Dori really digs my brother."

Cindy said, "She likes being with older kids. She'd be in love no matter who she was with."

"But you like Sam, don't you?"

"Of course. Don't you? Sam's a really nice kid."

"He's nice, and he lets people push him around."

"He's young. Sam will toughen up." She watched Sam and Dori move along the beach, disappearing into the mist.

Mark grinned, moving closer. In the dying firelight, his face was dark, his teeth white. He ran his hand gently along her arm. She looked into his face. He pressed his body against hers, kissing her lips,

A Quiet Place

moving his hand to unbutton her shirt. She pushed away. "I can't, Mark. Not now."

He rolled closer and hung above her, resting his weight on the palms of his hands. "Let's go walking. Back in the dunes."

She sat up, forcing one of his arms aside. "I want to go slow," she said.

He knelt, facing her, his eyes bright. "I like you, Cindy. I really do."

"I can't be like that. I've only known you a couple of weeks."

He nodded shortly, fumbled in a pocket of his shirt. He pulled out a little metal box. He said, "Let's have a joint."

Cindy looked off toward the water.

He said, "They'll be away long enough for us to smoke."

"I was busted before I started."

"Yeah, I bet."

"It's the truth," she said. "In New York. I was visiting a friend uptown. We went for a walk. We talked to some boys. One of them asked us if we wanted some grass."

Mark lit his joint. The sweet smell drifted away on the breeze. "Go ahead," he said.

A Quiet Place

"They took us to a tenement. We waited in the hall while they went upstairs. One of them came back with a little paper bag. We bought a little pinch of grass, barely enough for one joint."

Mark exhaled a thin stream of smoke. "Then what happened?"

"A couple of cops had been watching us. They packed all three of us into their car. Took us to the station house."

"And then?"

"They called our parents. My father came first. He was white as a ghost." She picked up a fistful of sand, let it trickle through her fingers. "We were allowed to go home with our parents. My friend and I. The boy spent the night in jail. The cops couldn't find his parents."

Mark smiled.

She looked toward him anxiously, eyes shining. "Don't tell anyone about it, will you?"

He sucked at his joint. "OK," he said.

"Promise?"

"Sure. When were you busted?"

"Three years ago."

"How old are you now?"

"Seventeen."

A Quiet Place

He whistled softly. "Barely out of your cradle. How old was the boy who sold you the stuff?"

"I can't remember. Older than we were. He was nice. He was fronting for some older men. That's what he said when he talked to the cops."

"Sounds as if the boy was a jerk."

Cindy stared into the mist. She said, "Remember this is our secret. Don't forget."

"Afraid Ike Thorne might hear about it?"

"Leave Ike Thorne out of this. Of course I wouldn't want the Thornes to know. Or anyone else."

"Of course," he said. "I understand that." He propped himself up on one of his elbows. "Don't be so touchy."

She looked toward the bluff. The lone car was almost lost in the shadows, dark and a little forbidding. She spoke softly. "I know I'm touchy about the Thornes. It's just that they could be hurt so easily. At least it seems that way to me. Ike Thorne can take care of himself. In a way he's tough. And his parents are, too. They have plenty of courage. But leading a country life as they have. . . ."

Mark nodded and offered her his joint. She shook

A Quiet Place

her head. He put his lips against it and took a short puff.

She went on. "They're happy. Happy being what they are. They're intelligent people. But if they heard about a thing like that, that I'd had trouble with the police. . . ."

Headlights flashed at the top of the dunes. As the car drew up to the abyss, its driver left the headlights burning. Mark stiffened.

Cindy said, "What's the matter?"

"Speak of the devil."

He dug a little pit in the sand, flicked off the burning end of the joint, reached for the metal box, put in the butt, and closed the box. A uniformed man moved across the parking lot, toward the shadowy car at the end of the lot.

Mark tossed the box into the pit, filled it in, and dusted it over with dry sand. He took a twig from beside the fire and marked the place where the box was buried.

The voice of the policeman, talking to the people in the car, sounded a high, metallic note, fading with the rising hiss of the sea. The headlights of the car went on. The starter racketed, the engine fired,

A Quiet Place

and the car backed around. It moved slowly into the night.

Mark said, "Why can't they leave them alone? Where can they go?" He rasped, "Move along, kids. Home to Mama." He stood up. "Love isn't legal in this state. Legislature passed a bill in 1830. No sporting events on Sunday." He added in a low voice, "Except for people over forty."

5

The policeman stood, hands on hips, looking toward them, a silhouette. He shouted, "How many of you down there?"

Mark faced the ocean, saying nothing. The man came nearer, walking in the sand, shining a flashlight in their direction. The other car door slammed. The first policeman stopped. The voice of the second rose above the sound of the sea, hollow, splitting the summer air. "Did you hear the sergeant ask a question?"

Mark said tensely, "Giving us the bullhorn treatment now." He turned and, cupping his hands around his mouth, yelled, "There are six of us."

A Quiet Place

Both policemen moved toward them. Mark said, under his breath, "Makes me think of those World War II movies. They're defending their lonely island beach."

The man with the bullhorn said, "What are you doing here?"

Mark said with an edge in his voice, "We were having a picnic."

"Where are the others?"

"My younger brother went walking with his date. A friend of mine took my sister for a walk."

"Which of you is driving the Massachusetts car?"

"My friend," Mark said.

"I want to see your licenses and registrations."

Mark cupped his hands again. He called out to his brother and sister.

The sergeant gestured toward Cindy. "This your girl?"

"She's a friend," Mark said.

A frightened voice came out of the mist. "Mark? That you? What's the trouble?"

"No trouble. Have you seen David?"

Sam and Dori came closer, Dori hanging back. "Who's that you're with?"

A Quiet Place

"A couple of cops."

"What do they want, Mark? What's the trouble."

The sergeant said, "Are any of you carrying drugs?"

Mark said, "No."

The sergeant tilted his light upward. He gave Sam a fisheye stare. "Are you the driver of the Massachusetts car?"

"No," Sam said in a shaking voice. "I don't have my license yet."

There were sounds beyond the dying fire. The sergeant brought his flashlight around. He caught David and Ann in a blaze of light, Ann covering her face. Mark said, "Take the light out of my sister's eyes."

The man lowered the light, and David moved forward with Ann beside him. Mark said, "I hope the registration is in the jeep. It belongs to my father. Here's my license." The sergeant looked at the license and handed it back. David fumbled in his wallet. He held out his license and registration. The sergeant asked, "Are you carrying drugs?"

David said, "No."

A Quiet Place

The man with the bullhorn said, "Do you know there's a curfew on this beach?"

Sam said, "No. We didn't know that. Never was a curfew here before."

The sergeant faced Mark. "How about you? Do know there's a curfew at sunset here?"

"I heard they planned to make it off limits after dark. Didn't know if they'd done it yet."

The sergeant raised his flashlight again. The beam struck Mark in the middle of the chest, lighting his features from underneath. The sergeant asked, "Were you in the service?"

Mark said hotly, "I'm fed up with this. Who in hell do you think you are? I was in the service. Now I'm in college. Back in college again."

The sergeant said, "Pick up your litter. He turned and started back toward the bluff, the other beside him, swinging the bullhorn, clicking its switch, rubbing his finger across the mouthpiece, making the instrument cackle and spit.

Dori's voice was shaking. "Why were they so mean to us?"

Sam said softly, "It's all right, Dori."

"Why were the policemen mean like that?"

A Quiet Place

Mark said, "Constipation maybe. The sergeant was probably constipated."

Dori started picking up their picnic things. Cindy knelt. Her hand went out. She said, "I think I left something here in the sand." She found the tin box and slipped it into one of her pockets.

The police car was turning away, its taillights red above the bluff. David and Ann had already left. Sam and Dori waited in the jeep.

The sound of the sea rose against the stillness. Three waves broke, one after the other; then a hush fell on the scene. Mark moved up beside Cindy. He said, "I sometimes imagine it without men, the sea and forests, the plains and canyons. How much better it would be without men."

"I hate to think of it with no one to enjoy it."

When they passed Speare's, the place was deserted. Mark was silent, eyes front, driving fast. Sam and Dori huddled together, keeping warm. Mark flicked a switch under the dashboard. Instant music flooded the night, a rhythmic beat, a complaining song. The engine howled; the air rushed against their faces.

As they approached the bridge, the jeep rocked, rounding the sharply banked curve, plummeting

A Quiet Place

down toward the open wooden structure. The tires slammed against the planks, changing the sound of passage. Sam shouted above the noise, "Slow down, Mark. For God's sake."

Cindy found the edges of her seat. She hung on. As they hit the blacktop on the far side, Mark swerved, braking at the same time. Dori screamed.

The jeep skidded to an uncertain stop. Mark turned around, attacking Dori. "Cut the screaming, will you, kid?"

Dori started crying softly. Sam said, "Let's go, but take it easy."

Cindy said softly, "You're half-stoned. You really better take it easy."

Mark stopped in front of the house. Sam said, "I'll take Dori to her door. Good night, Cindy."

Mark said, "Cindy's staying with us tonight."

"That's right. I forgot."

The jeep coasted along the street, under the shadows of the trees. It tilted into the gutter. Mark turned the key. The engine shuddered violently and died. Cindy said, "Forgive me, Mark. I want to go home."

Mark was silent.

A Quiet Place

"I didn't bring my toothbrush."

"Plenty of toothbrushes inside. Mother has extra ones for guests."

Cindy shook her head. She said, "I'm tired. I want to sleep in my own bed."

"Tonight was a mess. I know it was a mess."

Cindy touched the sleeve of Mark's jacket. "You're a great guy, Mark. You're not a nice guy, but you're great."

Sam walked behind the jeep, kicking up pebbles, slanting up the lawn toward the kitchen door, toward the yellow light inside.

Mark said, "I can't figure you at all." He put the tips of his fingers against her face and kissed her lightly on the mouth. He started the engine going again.

When he left her at the mailbox, he said, "You're not the bird for Ike Thorne. You and I are just summerfolk."

6

Cindy pulled up her blanket, tucking it over a bare shoulder. The sky outside was touched with pink. "Sunday," she whispered. She lay on her back staring at the ceiling.

She flicked the covers back and swung her legs over the side of the bed, reaching for her woolen bathrobe. On a table by the bed was a stack of paperback books, Herman Hesse's *Demian* on top. Beside a pair of sunglasses, propped against a lamp, was a standing mouse, made of cloth, wearing exquisitely hand-sewn garments, a little cap, a dress with tiny flowers on it, and a white apron fringed with lace. Cindy extended a forefinger and, advancing slowly, touched the tip of the mouse's nose.

She slipped her feet into her sandals and went into the bathroom, leaving the door ajar. She opened the door before she finished her teeth, walking into the living room, brushing as she looked around. She stood still, facing the windows on the bay side, then turned back to the bathroom, rinsed her mouth, and plunged her toothbrush into the rack.

She knelt on the couch, leaning on its back, facing the bay. As she opened the window, the morning air stung her lungs. The hayrick stood alone as if on a mountain crag, nothing behind it but a sea of mist. The sky above it was flaming orange, dipping to red before it melted into mist. Strung out against the sky were thin, horizontal clouds. The grass close by, the distant clouds—all seemed frozen, motionless.

Cindy unhooked the window screen. She let it slide down to the ground. She leaned on the windowsill, as if waiting for a sound, a sign of life. All at once a gull, a speck at first, appeared in the west and slowly, silently made its way across the stillness of the sky.

A Quiet Place

The mist became thinner above the pines. A patch of water flashed in the sun.

Cindy turned on the lamp on her father's writing table. She looked at her watch, went to her room, flung off her nightgown, and dressed quickly. She put on a heavy sweater and pulled it down around her hips.

She poured herself a tumbler of milk, cut a fat slice of oatmeal bread, and spread it with honey. She took a bite of the bread, gulped her milk, and moved toward the door. She stopped at her father's writing table. In the middle was a yellow legal pad. She wrote something on the pad.

Brindle jumped down sleepily from a chair. Cindy whispered, "Good morning, Brindle."

She put kibbles into his bowl and went out, closing the outside door behind her.

She moved fast, running now and then, alone on the ridge above the bay. A breeze had sprung up. The sky was violet, studded with racing, changing clouds. She moved through a deep pine forest, frightening a crow where he feasted on the carcass of a young raccoon. The animal's tail lay on a carpet of clover, its fur rippling in the morning air.

She mounted a second ridge, above the first, going

A Quiet Place

toward a white farmhouse with a barn behind it, black with age, its roof sagging like a nag's back. A big dog, white and ugly, loomed up in the middle of the road, lowering his head, barking and growling as Cindy came close. She spoke to him, and he slunk off, turning his head to growl again.

She walked fast past a cluster of farms, trucks standing in front of their barns, a flock of sheep gray against a white wall. She turned into the Thornes' driveway, looking first toward the house. A light burned in the kitchen window. It paled in the face of the brightening sky.

She turned toward the barn, and as she did so, the kitchen door opened. Ike came out. When he saw her, he shouted. He grinned and waved as he came down the steps. The door opened again, and Mrs. Thorne came out. She looked over a pair of reading glasses. "Goodness, Ike. What's the matter?" She smiled when she saw Cindy. "Why, Cindy. Whatever brought you here so early?"

"Couldn't sleep. And it's a fine morning."

Mrs. Thorne smoothed her apron. "I'll set another place for breakfast."

Ike and Cindy went to the barn. When Cindy finished milking Daisy, she half filled the pail with

A Quiet Place

the nipple at the bottom and held it while the calf chomped. She asked Ike, "You're sure this calf isn't going for veal?"

"I told you, Cindy. Her mother here is a prize cow. She won't go for veal."

"But she'll be leaving soon."

"I have no room for another cow. Maybe you should take her with you."

"She wouldn't be happy in a city apartment."

"Likely the neighbors would complain."

Ike finished milking Buttercup. He moved the pail aside, stood up, and leaned against the tie room wall. "When does school begin?" he asked.

"Later than it does here. I can't remember the date."

Ike nodded. He turned to the window, looking out, a brooding look.

They went to the house, down to the cellar, where Ike separated the milk. When he finished, they carried the pails to the kitchen. Mr. Thorne was already sitting at the table, his cane looped over the back of his chair. His face was thin and white, his cheeks shining. Cindy said, "Hello."

Mr. Thorne said, teasing, "Summerfolk are gen'ally late sleepers."

A Quiet Place

"I am mostly, "Cindy said. "But now and then, when I'm excited, I wake up early. I stay awake because life seems too good to miss."

Mr. Thorne said, "Life *is* too good to miss."

Ike said, "He means it, too. Last winter nearly killed him. And Grandpa and Grandma, too." He turned to Cindy, "You heard about Father's accident?"

Cindy said, "And your grandfather's operation. Must have kept the women busy."

Mrs. Thorne said, "We ran a hospital. Sure enough."

Ike said, "It was some winter."

Mrs. Thorne said, remembering, "But we've had worse winters. It was cold last winter, and the snow was deep; but winter's aren't as bad as they used to be."

"These are lovely pancakes," Cindy said.

"I made them for you, dear. It's been a wonderful blueberry year."

Ike was looking down at his napkin ring. It was bright-red plastic. He turned it over in his hand, then spun it on his index finger. His father said, "What the devil's eatin' you, boy?"

Ike put the napkin ring down. He looked up,

A Quiet Place

straight into his father's eyes. "Mother started me thinkin', that's all. Last winter I was finishing school. Up early, chores to do, off to school and back again. More chores. I was tired sometimes but never lonely." He touched his napkin ring again, turned it slowly on the tablecloth. He said deliberately, "Some of our neighbors look down on the summerfolk. But I don't see that at all." He looked at Cindy then back at the tablecloth. "Take Cindy here." His voice was low. "In some ways we're different, but in many we're the same. We both like animals." He stopped. "You like animals, don't you, Cindy?"

"I certainly do. You know I do."

Ike spread his hands against the table, palms down, forcing his thumbs toward each other. "Well, I like company," he said. He brightened. "Animals are fine, but I ain't married to any of 'em."

Mrs. Thorne said, "When will you be leaving, Cindy?"

"We're leaving Thursday."

Mrs. Thorne said, "Would you like to stay on with us a while?"

Mr. Thorne's eyes brightened. "Why not?" he said. "Extend your vacation a week or so."

Ike beamed. "If she stays, she works."

A Quiet Place

Mrs. Thorne got up and went to the stove. "Have some more," she said. "There's plenty of batter."

Cindy said, "I'd like to stay a few days more. I really would. I'll think about it. And ask my father if I can."

Ike glanced up at the kitchen clock. "I better take some milk to Mia Sears. Want to come along, Cindy?"

Cindy nodded. "After that I better go home. I've been neglecting my Dad."

Mrs. Thorne said, "And take a couple of dozen eggs." She turned to Cindy. "Come on back for Sunday dinner. Mother and Father would like to see you."

"I better not. I'll see them next week if I stay on with you."

As they walked to the truck, Ike did a little dance, grinning at Cindy. She said, "Watch out. You'll spill the milk."

"Mind the eggs," he said. "Don't you worry about the milk."

7

Mia Sears came out to greet them. Ike said, "You remember Cindy. Cindy's helping us at the farm. She's a volunteer."

Mia was young and small-boned. She took Cindy's hand. "Good to see you again," she said. "Summer's a good time to be in Maine." She looked up at Ike. "You got a minute, Ike? Ben's having trouble with our heifer. She's off her feed. Thin as a rail. And he'd like to ask you about our pump. It doesn't shut itself off."

"Tank must be waterlogged," Ike said. "Got to drain 'er. Or pump in a cushion of air. Nothing to worry about there."

A Quiet Place

Ike moved toward the ramshackle barn. He rolled a little when he walked, like a drunken sailor. Cindy watched him admiringly. "Just finished school last spring," she said. "Who could believe that he just finished school? When I first met Ike, I thought he was twenty-four or -five."

"He never had much time for play. He no sooner finished school than the accident put his father out of service." Mia smiled. "But he always has time to help his neighbors."

As Cindy and Mia approached the house, a small boy come out howling and gurgling. He yelled, "Jenny kicked me. Tell her to stop it, will you, Mom?"

"Tell her yourself, dear."

The child advanced and grabbed his mother's skirt. He was wearing a filthy Micky Mouse shirt with orange juice dribbled down its front. He let go of his mother and gurgled again, more like a baby than a walking child. Mia said, "Stevie, look what you've done to your shirt." She sighed, patting the child's belly. "Orange juice belongs inside."

The child started sucking at the stained cloth. His mother trembled as she reached for his arm. "Stop it, Stevie. Please stop it. Go find your father and Mr. Thorne. Mr. Thorne is helping him with the heifer."

The child ran off. "What a mercy," Mia said. "Sometimes he goes on like that for hours. Would you like some coffee?"

"I would."

A large poster hung on the kitchen wall, a photograph of a delicate tree. Most of the leaves were sunlit yellow, against an expanse of gray rock. Cindy said, "What a beautiful photograph."

Mia rummaged in a pile of dirty dishes. She found two mugs, rinsed them under the faucet, and dried them with a tattered towel. She poured the coffee. Her face was like the face of a child. "It is," she said. "I'm glad you like it. It's a comfort to me on winter days."

"The leaves are like the leaves in a painting by Corot."

The woman's eyes were bright. "You must know something about painting. I studied painting before I married Ben. I studied in Paris when I was young. And I did some drawings in France years later when I went there with Ben." She took a sip of coffee. "I was hoping to do some painting here." She

A Quiet Place

brushed her hand across her forehead. "But I hardly ever paint anymore at all."

Cindy stirred her coffee, watching the whirlpool grow deep. "You have to get away," she said. "You have to get away sometimes."

Mia nodded solemnly. "I do. I go down to Boston. We both came from Boston, you know. I go down to the art museums. And when I come back, I want to paint. I do paint, too. When I come back from Boston, I sometimes paint."

They could hear Ike's voice in the yard. He was talking about the water pump, joking and teasing Ben Sears.

Cindy said, "I'd like to see your work."

"I don't like to show it. I haven't done anything really good. I paint for pleasure." She turned and looked up at the poster again. "What do you plan to do with your life?"

Cindy laughed. "I wish I could say. Or maybe I don't. Wish I could say, that is. I suppose I'm like a lot of other girls. I like to read. I write poetry once in a while." She held out her cup for more coffee. "I wanted to write about the sunrise this morning. But I didn't. I went to visit the Thornes instead."

A Quiet Place

She sipped her coffee. "I should probably be angrier than I am."

"What do you mean?"

"To write good things you have to be passionate. Or bitter, or both. A lot of kids my age are bitter. I can see what makes them bitter, but I can't feel bitterness in myself."

Mrs. Sears gave Cindy a searching look, fussed with the handle of the coffeepot. "That's the way my husband is." She looked out the screen door. "He's gentle and good. And unworldly. If everyone was like him, there'd be no war." She added shyly, "I'm that way, too. But not as much as Ben."

The screen door squeaked, and Ike came through, his tall body blocking the dappled light in the front yard. He was followed by the slight form of Mr. Sears. Ike said, "You remember Ben Sears."

Mr. Sears smiled shyly, taking Cindy's hand. He said, "How do you do?"

Ike said, "Cindy, we better be moving on."

A girl, a year or so older than her brother, came banging downstairs. She said, in a matter-of-fact way, "Stevie's in the hayloft. I just saw him poking his head out."

Mia Sears shot out of the door, Ike and Mr. Sears

behind her. Cindy followed. Ike stood under the gaping doorway while his parents went in to bring the child out. Ike said sternly, "Move away from the edge."

The boy obeyed, but when he heard his parents' voices behind him, he moved toward the edge again. Ike stood alert, until Mia caught the boy's arm and pulled him back.

Ike grinned down at Cindy. He shook his head. "What would you have done if he'd fallen?"

"I'd have caught him."

"He might have broken your back."

"Not likely," Ike said. "He can't weigh as much as a full-grown sow."

Cindy laughed. "Did you ever play catch with a full-grown sow?"

"Don't s'pose I ever did."

The truck whacked into a pothole as it turned out the driveway. Ike said, "Ouch. Pay attention, boy."

Cindy said, "Does the Sears family have a chance?"

"Ben Sears has some money of his own. But they'll never make farmers if that's what you mean. Look

A Quiet Place

at us. I don't sit around much. Maybe you noticed. And Father worked at the ironworks fourteen years." Ike gave Cindy a sly glance. " 'Course Father's a rich man, you know."

"No, I mean it. If he'd sell off some land, we'd have money to burn. We have close to a hundred acres."

"When it's yours, will you sell it?"

"Not if I can help it. I love this place. It's been in the family since the seventeen hundreds."

"I don't suppose I'd sell it either."

"But we might have to to keep going. You can't make a living farming here. Haven't been able to for fifty years in spite of what the old-timers say. Why do you suppose my father went to work?" He slapped the wheel. "And it's a good thing he did. Now that he's laid up, the union helps him. Father would like to do away with unions, but the unions help him all the same."

"You father's quite a man. Full of intelligence and wit."

"He is."

"Why would he like to do away with unions?"

"Father would like to roll the clock back. To a time when a farm could support a family. So would

A Quiet Place

I when it comes to that. I was born a farmer. I'll die one, too."

The truck rolled along the high ridge. The sun was bright. The trees cast deep shadows. A single sail flashed above the surface of the bay. Ike left her at the mailbox. He looked at his watch. "Home in plenty of time for lunch."

"It is morning still? Seems like midafternoon to me."

"Your father's sure to let you stay awhile after he leaves."

She climbed down from the truck. "Yes, I think so." She slammed the truck door. She said, "Thank your mother for the pancakes."

8

The sky was filled with darkening, swiftly moving clouds. As Mark swerved onto the exit ramp, the moon appeared, dead ahead, a thin crescent. Cindy said, "Like to a silver bow new bent in heaven...."

"A scholar," he said.

"Not much of a scholar. An aspiring poet."

"Isn't every girl an aspiring poet?"

"Of course."

He gave her a half-smile. "When are you leaving for the big city?"

"My father leaves tomorrow morning. Mrs. Thorne asked me to stay on with them."

The headlights picked out a road sign, white

A Quiet Place

luminescence against the dark. Mark swung left on a blacktop road. As they passed a tavern, a candlelit place with colonial pretensions, Mark said, "When Mother gave me the tickets, I should have said no."

"I've forgotten the story. I must've been six when I saw the movie. I'd like to see the play. Suffer through it with me."

"It's not the show that puts me off. It's all those women in tight, gray curls, all those dressed-up middle-aged people." He smiled to himself, turning again to look at Cindy. "It's worth it, though, just to see you dressed up. Cindy in a long skirt. And I like the little bag. Where'd you get the bag?"

"My sister made it for me. I really love it."

"How old is your sister?"

"Twenty-two. She's a good person, really good."

They drove along a quiet stretch of road and crossed a thoroughfare, bursting into a brightly lighted section of road, lined with curb service places, bars, and bowling alleys. They took the middle lane, avoiding a clot of cars waiting at the entrance to a drive-in theater. "I hate that kind of thing," he said.

"What kind of thing?"

"Mass lovemaking. Now line up here, and when

A Quiet Place

you park inside, park in a line, side by side. And then you make love by the numbers."

"I don't like it much either. But how about the kids who have no place to go, like the kids we saw parked out on Bass Island?"

He gestured toward the drive-in. "They can line up if they want to. I don't like it. You wouldn't either if you'd been in the army."

She said, "Who's touchy now?"

He slammed on the brakes as they approached a traffic light. "I'm touchy," he said, between clenched teeth.

They drove into a quiet campus, shade trees along the road, old buildings, most of them dark, soft shadows and yellow lamps on black columns. They parked at an angle, parallel to other cars. Cindy started to speak, but she saw Mark's face, grave and unyielding. They climbed down from the jeep, faced the network of winding walks.

Across the quadrangle, the theater was alive, its windows radiating light, the people in front knotted together, talking and waiting, some of them around a refreshment stand under a brightly striped awning.

As they moved toward the theater, he said, "We

A Quiet Place

have time to kill. Did you ever go to the art museum here? There's a Rembrandt there and an early Wyeth. I think there's a Corot. I can't remember. When you've seen one Corot, you've seen them all."

As they left the museum, the crowd was funneling into the theater.

The theater was crowded. Men in suits, white shirts and striped ties talked to men in striped shirts and quiet ties. Powdered women smiled at each other. Mark and Cindy found their seats. Mark whispered, "Wednesday night at the Sphere in the Cube Theater the leading citizens of Zonk County gathered to watch a first-rate performance...."

Cindy said, "I'm sick of hearing you sound off."

His eyes flashed. "Let's get out of here."

"Give me my stub. Go if you want to."

The houselights dimmed. The buzz of talk became a murmur. Mark sat back, propping his knees against the seat in front of him.

At the final curtain the audience applauded. There were curtain calls. Mark dove for a side exit, pulling Cindy behind him. Outside, a light rain was falling. She said, "I loved it."

A Quiet Place

"It's dated," Mark said. "But it's a good show."

As they hurried toward the jeep, he said, "You're OK."

"What brought that on?"

"I don't know. At first I thought you were a Pollyanna."

"What's a Pollyanna?"

"Someone who thinks things are just dandy. They like their parents, and they like the police. They like apple pie."

"I suppose I am a Pollyanna. I like my parents even though they don't like each other. The cops who busted me were great guys. They were kind and understanding. And hot apple pie is one of my favorites."

"But sometimes parents are impossible, cold and insensitive. Sergeant Zilch who kicked us off the beach was a son of a bitch. And cold, commercial apple pies are barely fit for human consumption. You remember the bright side. I remember the dark." They got to the jeep. Mark started to raise the top. He said, "But you're not really a Pollyanna."

As they crossed a bridge, water running fast a hundred feet below, the rain came harder, sweeping

A Quiet Place

into the jeep on Cindy's side. She leaned toward him and he put his hand on hers, holding it tight. He said, "How about stopping at our place?"

"What time is it?"

"Must be about eleven. Stop for a while. David went back home this morning. But Sam invited Dori to come for supper. Let's go in and play some records."

"OK."

They ran from the jeep to the front door. As they entered the hall, they heard laughter in the living room. A man's voice hailed them, and they looked in. Mark's father, short and balding, offered his hand. "You're Cindy. I remember."

Mark's mother was holding a glass in her hand. She shifted her weight unsteadily, said, "Hello there, Cindy. Did you have a good time?"

Cindy said, "We really enjoyed it. I'm certainly glad you gave us the tickets."

Mark's mother waved toward the couple sitting on the couch. The man rose to his feet. Mark's mother said, "These are the Carlsens."

"I've met Mrs. Carlsen. How do you do."

Mr. Carlsen sat down again.

Mark was standing in the doorway. He said,

A Quiet Place

"Cindy lost a sweater the other night. We thought it might be here. We just stopped by to see if we can find it."

Mark's father's voice was suddenly loud. "Have a drink before you go. Why doesn't everybody have a drink?" He turned to Mrs. Carlsen, who was backed against the cushions like a wingless bird. She said, "I better not have another."

Mr. Carlsen pushed his glass toward Mark's father, who took it, turning to talk to Cindy. "Well now, Cindy, how about it?"

Mark broke in. "I told Cindy's father I'd bring her home early."

Mark's father winked broadly. "Go along and look for the sweater."

"What did it look like?" Mark's mother asked.

Cindy said, "It was the color of natural wool." She followed Mark toward the back of the hall. Mark rummaged in the coat closet. Under his breath, he said, "Goddam." He handed her an old raincoat. "Take this," he said.

"Thanks," she whispered. "What a liar you are! Do you think they believed I left a sweater here?"

He said, loud enough for his parents to hear, "Go back to the sunporch and see if it's there."

A Quiet Place

When she came back, Mark was standing by the door. He'd taken off his tie and put on a worn and dirty raincoat. The rain was falling lightly now. As they moved toward the jeep, Sam and Dori came out of the darkness. Sam said, "Hi. Mom and Dad in there?"

Mark said, "They're sitting in there with the Carlsens. They're all half-bombed. Why don't you go back to Dori's house?"

Dori said, "Do you think we should?"

"Yes, I think you should. I think that's exactly what you should do."

As Mark started the jeep, he said, "I wish the roof didn't leak so much."

"You frightened poor Dori half to death."

"I suppose I did. Someone better frighten her before it's too late."

Cindy laughed. "What's that supposed to mean?"

"Damned if I know. It's one of those cryptic remarks of mine. Meant to veil my honest simplicity."

They stopped at the light at the edge of the village. "I'm taking you home," he said. "No sense driving around in the rain."

"After I leave, you'll write me, won't you?"

"I guess so," he said.

59

A Quiet Place

"Mark, please. I want you to write."

When they came to the mailbox, Mark said, "I'll leave you here. Say goodbye to your father for me." He kissed the corner of her mouth. She reached for a handhold and jumped down, started to move away. She stopped abruptly and turned back. He slid across the right front seat and jumped out of the jeep. He took her in his arms, rocking her body back and forth, kissing her neck. A truck's engine sounded in the distance. The truck came closer. The mailbox and the trees behind it were suddenly flooded with yellow light. Cindy turned away from Mark. The truck slowed as it passed the jeep. It's taillights grew smaller as it moved away.

Mark said, "Any chance of another date?"

"I can't, Mark. You know I can't. Starting tomorrow, I'll be the Thornes' guest."

9

Her father stood by the car, hands on hips, looking up at the luggage rack. He stepped forward and tightened a knot.

Cindy was sitting on the doorstep, holding Brindle, hugging him and kissing him around his ears. Her father moved over and sat beside her, looking toward the bay. He said, "I hate to leave. It's selfish, but I wish you were going with me."

"I'll be starting back soon, in a week at most."

"I don't much like the end of summer." He stood up and went into the house.

Cindy got up as he came back out. He said, "Is your bag in the car?"

A Quiet Place

"It's there, Papa. There's not much in it. I won't need much. Most of my stuff is in the carton. I put my guitar in the back seat."

"You haven't called me Papa since you were a kid." He put his arm around her shoulder. "You're quiet this morning. Everything all right?"

"I'm thinking," she said. "I have some things to think about."

They got into the car and slammed the doors. As they turned into the road, Cindy said, "Remember to leave the keys in the village."

"I will."

Mrs. Thorne was outside when they arrived. She came to meet them. She said, "Ike's down at Finger Point setting a splint on the Browns' cow." She turned to Cindy's father, her eyes steady. "I'm glad Cindy can stay awhile. She's taken to farming like a duck to water. And we like to have her with us. She's company for Ike. And Mr. Thorne and me."

Cindy reached back for her suitcase. Brindle wagged his tail, then sat, watching her anxiously. Cindy's father said, "It's good of you to have her. Cindy's not really a city girl, you know. We lived in the country until she was twelve."

Mrs. Thorne said, "Can I help you, dear?"

A Quiet Place

"No, thanks. I'm only keeping this one small bag."

"How about the guitar? Isn't that yours?"

"I think I'll let my father take it back to the city."

"I love the sound of a guitar."

"I only know four or five songs." She turned, looking at the woman's face, then back at her guitar. The wood was dark, the strings and frets glinting in the morning light. She said, "I'll keep it if you like. I brought it along and never played it."

"You'll certainly have an audience here."

* * *

Mr. Thorne got up from the table. He went to the living room, walking carefully, using his cane. He crowed happily, "Good supper. Good to have you here, Cindy."

Cindy started helping with the dishes, but Ike said, "Let her off tonight, will you, Mother? Let her come with me to the barn."

"You'd think I meant to keep the girl a prisoner. She's free to go anywhere she likes."

Cindy said, "I'll help you put the things in the washer. It won't take a minute."

He winked at Cindy. "If Ma will let you, you can come along when you finish helping."

A Quiet Place

His mother turned in mock annoyance. Ike reached out and grabbed her arm, pulling her toward him, picking her up and swinging her around. Her cheeks were flushed. She said, "Goodness, Ike. Save your hugging for the girls at the grange."

"None of them are as pretty as you."

He put her down and she faced Cindy, wiping her hands of her apron. "Listen to him. His father was like that when he was young. Full of compliments."

Mr. Thorne shouted from the next room, "Still am." He laughed. "Now you run along and stop pestering your mother."

The television set went on, bringing hollow voices into the house, streaking the doorframe with blue light.

When Cindy finished in the kitchen, she pushed out the screen door. The night was chilly, stars shining. A thin yellow light around the barn doors, a streak of light from the tie room window, added weight to the bulk of the barn. A bell tinkled in the pasture. Cindy stood a minute, listening. She heard the clank of a tool against heavier metal. She moved into the barn. Ike was working on the tractor engine. He said, "Damn this plug. Can't take it out. One of 'em isn't firing right. I think it's this one."

A Quiet Place

The work light shone into his face. His cheeks were pink, his eyes bright. He seemed on the verge of smiling. "Father taught me about engines. Guess I told you that. Poor old Father. He's full of dreams."

"Dreams keep us going. What would we be without our dreams?"

"Not me. It's work keeps me going. It's the farm that keeps me happy."

"You must have dreams."

He half turned in her direction, keeping a hand on the wrench he was using. He nodded slowly. "I suppose I do."

"What kind of dreams does your father have?"

"You know that old lobster boat in the yard?"

"Yes."

"That's the skeleton of one of Father's dreams."

"That's a sad and poetic thing to say."

"Well, it's true. He wanted to have a lobster fleet. That boat was to have been the first. Never put out a pot. Not even one. As for me, I never heard the call of the sea. I like to feel the land under my feet. I like to watch the oxen obey my commands. I like to play midwife to the cows. Did you ever see the oxen perform?"

A Quiet Place

"No, I never did."

"We'll put them through their paces tomorrow morning. There's a pile of logs across the road. Back in among the trees. We'll fetch them and stack them alongside the shed. I'll split them and cut them in the fall." He reached for a hammer and tapped the wrench handle. "You ever been to a country fair?"

She shook her head. "I've always wanted to go to one."

He put the hammer and wrench down and raised the work light, looking for something. He picked up an oil can and pushed the light toward Cindy. "Pull up that barrel and sit down."

She did as she was told.

He said, "There's plenty of fairs this time of year. We'll look at the paper when we go inside. We'll pick a fair and show the team. Did you know they won three blue ribbons already?"

"I never knew you'd shown them."

"Well, I did." He tapped the wrench with the hammer again. "There she comes. Should've oiled her before. Only thing is you got to keep the plugs dry."

"You seem to know a lot about engines. Your father must have been a good teacher."

A Quiet Place

"Don't know much. Just the basics. Father's the one who knows about engines."

"Why is it women don't learn about engines?"

"It's custom, I guess. Some of them do. Best mechanic in the state is a woman in Brunswick." He pursed his lips. " 'Course she does look more like a man than a woman. Wears a denim engineer's cap and an oversized set of coveralls."

"You can't expect her to work in a skirt."

Ike held the spark plug in his hand. He dried it with a clean rag and held it to the light. He tapped the end of it with the hammer and held it against the light again. He said, "There."

Cindy asked, "Do you really need the oxen? Can't a tractor do all the hauling?"

Ike smiled. He said, "That's a touchy question. People hereabouts tease me about them. They say my oxen are just for show. Take Henry. You met Henry. Henry says I should keep them in a heated stall, tie ribbons around their necks. In a way he's right about the oxen being for show." He smiled to himself, leaning over, holding the work light in his left hand, the spark plug in the other. "And in a way they're wrong. Take that pile of logs out there. Can't drive a tractor in among the trees." He

A Quiet Place

chuckled, looking around. "And what if they are just for show? Life should have its little pleasures."

"It certainly should."

"Father hasn't had much pleasure. Except, of course, being married to Mother." He straightened up looking at the tractor, half turned toward Cindy. He said, "Mother didn't mean it about the girls."

"About what girls?"

"The girls at the grange."

"What did she say about the girls at the grange?"

His color deepened. "She said I hugged the girls at the grange."

Cindy said, "Good grief, Ike. There's nothing wrong in that."

"I know," he said. "But I never even learned to dance."

She looked down at her feet, saying nothing. They heard a small sound at the barn door. She got up and let the Thornes' dog in. She sat beside Cindy, her tail thumping the rough floor. Cindy patted her, speaking softly. "Poor old thing. One of her eyes is growing white."

"She's losing her eyesight. Old age is often sad." He put the spark plug in, tightening it with the wrench. He asked, "Do you miss Brindle?"

A Quiet Place

"Not really. Not yet. I know I'll see him soon. I only miss people if they're dead. Or if I know I won't see them for a long time." She smiled. "Brindle's not exactly a person, but he often seems like one to me."

He wiped his hands and went to a shelf and put his tools away. As he came back, she stood up. He said, "Do you miss your mother?"

"Sometimes," she said. "I'm going to visit her at Christmas."

"Only one person I miss right now and that's Granddad. Father's father and I were friends. We often worked in the fields together. He had bright blue eyes and a ready wit." Ike compressed his lower lip. "I loved the old fella. And in the winter, when the roads were blocked, when the weather kept him by his fire, I never let a day go by but what I talked to him on the phone. Granddad gave me treasures I'll never lose."

"He must have been a fine man."

"He was. I miss calling him up. I think of something I want to tell him or ask him about, and then I remember I can't call him up." He turned off the work light. They went outside, the dog trailing si-

A Quiet Place

lently behind. He looked up at the stars. "I miss him most of all in July when we bring in the hay."

She said, "I've never lost anyone I loved that much."

They moved toward the house. He said, "Losing people is part of life."

10

The following day after lunch they brought the oxen out. Ike opened the gate, clucking and calling. The beasts stood facing them, ten feet or so apart, twitching their ears. Ike said, "Cindy, are you afraid of them?"

"No."

"Well, bring the younger one out. I'll get the other. Watch your feet. If one of 'em steps on you, you'll know it."

When the oxen stood together in the yard, Ike raised the wooden yoke. He lowered it to their necks and Cindy helped him put the oxbows on. Ike hitched the oxen to the stone boat. He shouted, and

A Quiet Place

they leaned forward, their massive shoulders gleaming in the sun. They moved toward the woodlot across the road. Ike shouted and whacked them when they failed to respond as he expected them to. He gave one of them a clout, with the flat of his hand, sending up a cloud of dust.

Cindy helped load the stone boat, and when it was full, Ike coaxed the oxen around, they crossed the road and unloaded the wood, stacking it by the side of the house. It took six trips to move the pile. As they led the oxen back to the gate, Ike said, "Good thing we don't cook with wood anymore. Or coal. In spite of how Father talks sometimes, things are better than when he was a boy."

Ike straightened up. Little drops of sweat clung to his upper lip. Cindy's face was flushed. He said, "Well, thanks, Cindy." He touched her cheek with a forefinger. "Work brings out the roses in your cheeks."

They went to the hen pen to gather eggs. Ike laughed when a hen cackled at her and rose up flapping, sending her reeling backward. He said, "There's a girl for you. Doesn't turn a hair when a nineteen-hundred-pound beast walks toward her, but a chicken sends her reeling backward."

A Quiet Place

"I don't like all those feathers. And they peck you when you reach for eggs. They seem such idiotic birds."

He reached for the hen, clapping his hand around her neck, turning her aside and reaching under. "That's true," he said. "A man wants a microscope to see their brains. Jus' one thing good about 'em." The hen squawked and pecked at his wrist. "Look what we've done now. We've hurt her feelin's." He took a swipe at a deerfly that lit on his cheek. He grinned. "Nothing's so good as an egg in the morning. Except maybe Mother's pancakes."

"And chickens are certainly good to eat."

He handed her the bucket with the eggs in it. He said, "Take these to Mother. And ask her to box a couple of dozen. I'll bring the truck around, and we'll take them to Mia Sears. They should have chickens of their own. Maybe I'll give them half a dozen chicks. Trouble is the children wouldn't leave them alone." He shook his head. "I swear I've never seen such a family. The kids do exactly as they please."

"I really like Mrs. Sears."

"I do too. And she likes you." He ran his hand

A Quiet Place

through his hair. "When it comes to that, I like them both."

Mrs. Thorne was in the kitchen. Cindy said, "Ike said to give you these. They're for Mrs. Sears."

Mrs. Thorne put the bucket by the sink. A bell rang. She picked up the phone. She said, "Hello, Nora."

Ike's footsteps sounded on the back steps. Mrs. Thorne said, "Goodness, Nora. That's too bad."

Ike came in, clucking in a teasing way. His mother put her hand over the mouthpiece. "You hush, Ike. It's Nora Smith."

"I figured as much."

Cindy took the eggs out of the bucket, one by one, washing the dirty ones, drying them on a dish towel. Mrs. Thorne said, "I'm sure he'd be glad to, Nora."

Ike made a face. He whispered. "Glad to. 'Course I am. I got nothing to do but doctor their cow."

Cindy frowned. Ike said, "I hope you know I'm joking."

Cindy said, "What? I'm sorry. I must have been thinking of something else."

"Just so you know I don't begrudge them my time."

"You're as generous a person as I've ever met."

A Quiet Place

Mrs. Thorne said, "Ike?"

"Tell her I'll be there in half an hour."

Mrs. Thorne said, "He'll be along soon. He planned to go down your way today. Good-bye, dear. Hope we'll see you before too long."

Ike said, "Planned to go down that way my eye."

"Ike, you stop it. She might have heard you."

"You'd hung up before I said it."

"Nevertheless."

Ike turned to Cindy. "What you doin' anyway? Look at the girl, Ma. She's washing Mia Sears' eggs."

"What's got into you today, Ike? You're fresh as paint. It's nice she's washing Mia's eggs."

Ike spoke softly. "It really is. And I've seen you do a thing or two for Mia. Sometimes you treat her like a child."

Mrs. Thorne opened two egg boxes and put them on the drainboard. Cindy dried her hands and put the eggs in the boxes. "Eggs always remind me of Easter. Do you ever decorate eggs at Easter?"

Ike said, "Mother does wonderful eggs at Easter."

His mother said, "And Mia. She does beautiful Easter eggs. Mia's an artist. I guess you know."

A Quiet Place

Ike said, "And Jenny and Stevie throw them at each other."

Mrs. Thorne laughed. "You're really a terror today, Ike." She looked wistfully toward Ike. "Yes, I remember painting eggs. When you were little. I used to like to paint eggs."

Cindy put the boxes one on top of the other. Ike held the screen door open. They moved into the sunshine toward the truck, Ike kicking happily at stones in the yard.

Mrs. Sears held out her hand. She said, "Come in, Cindy."

Cindy handed Mrs. Sears the eggs. Ike said, "She washed them for you."

Mrs. Sears smiled at Ike. "Ben and Stevie are in the barn. I think Jenny must be sleeping. She started napping hours ago. Maybe she's coming down with something."

Ike said gently, "Let her sleep."

When Ike had gone, Mrs. Sears said, "There's no finer man than Ike. He's strong, and he's the soul of kindness."

Cindy looked after him. She said in an almost in-

A Quiet Place

audible voice, "He certainly is. He's both those things."

"What is it, dear? You seem so sad." She straightened up. "Forgive me for asking. I was moody as could be when I was in my teens. And how I hated people who pried."

"It doesn't matter. You're not at all a prying person."

They went into the kitchen by the side door. Mrs. Sears put the eggs in the refrigerator. "It's not just Ike," she said. "It's all of them. They've been good to us."

Cindy looked up at the picture of the trees, the bright leaves against the rock. She said, "Mia. May I call you Mia?"

"Of course."

"When do you plan to go to the city?"

"I have no plans. I'd like to go, though. I haven't been away from here in six months."

"When I go, maybe you can come with me. It's time you went to a few museums."

"The paintings in Boston are all old friends. I'd like to see them again."

"Maybe you should come to New York. And make

new friends. How long has it been since you were in New York?"

"It's been a long time."

"You wouldn't know the Metropolitan. There's an esplanade with fountains on either side. They've bought new things. And the ones they had before are in different settings. And then there's the Whitney and the Frick. Have you been to those? And the galleries on Fifty-seventh Street."

Mia smiled. "I'd love to go with you. But Ben lets the children run rings around him." She sat down, looking toward the stove, then up at the picture of the trees. "I suppose I'd better go before winter sets in. In winter it's hard to get away." She looked slyly at Cindy. "Sit down. Coffee will be ready soon."

Mia filled the kettle and put it on the stove. "What made you ask me to go to New York? Just then, I mean."

"I guess I wasn't really thinking of you. I was thinking of myself. I didn't want to go back alone. And face the city. The city is a lonely place sometimes."

Mia's eyes were bright. "I think I'll go. I'll stay

A Quiet Place

with an old school friend of mine. I heard from her a week or so ago."

"What could be better?"

Mia suddenly looked like a girl in her teens. "Ben can manage for a few days."

Ike spoke through the screen door. "What are you girls cookin' up?" He spoke again, not waiting for an answer. "I got to move along to Finger Point. Jack Brown's cow is in need of attention." He chuckled. "Cindy, you finished cookin' up things? Do you want to come along with me?"

Cindy said, "I think I'll stay with Mia awhile."

"I'll stop by for you on my way back."

"I'll walk. I think I'd rather walk."

"See you back at the house."

11

She was walking away from the Sears' house, just rounding the first bend, when she heard the jeep coming toward her. She stepped out of the road and sat on a low stone wall, holding still, her eyes fixed on the road ahead. The jeep appeared at the next curve, going fast. Its right wheels were off the blacktop, running in the dry soil, kicking up a cloud of dust.

Mark braked when he saw her, his right wheels skidding, the left ones holding, so the front end swung away from Cindy. She stood up. "Why don't you grow up?" she said. "First thing you know you'll kill a child."

A Quiet Place

"Or a chicken."

She ignored him. "How would you like to have that on your conscience? Snuffing out the life of somebody's child?"

Mark grinned, sitting high in the driver's seat. She moved toward the side of the jeep. His grin disappeared. He rocked slightly and blinked sleepily. With sudden intensity he said, "I saw a dead child once."

"But you hadn't killed it."

"Someone else had. Someone had shot it."

She stared at the side of the jeep, at a place where the body had been dented. The metal was rusting where the paint had come off. She said, "What are you doing here, Mark?"

"I was looking for you."

"Did you go to the Thornes'?"

He pointed to a sweater on the seat beside him, a bright-red cardigan. "Yes, I did. I told them my mother had found this sweater. I said she thought it might be yours."

She said softly, "Please don't chase me. Write me when I'm back in the city."

"You want a pen pal, is that it?"

81

"You know damned well I can't see you here."

"Watch your language."

She looked back along the road. "Is this the only road to Finger Point?"

"As far as I know." He gave her a sly look. "Is Ike Thorne at Finger Point?"

"Yes, he is." She shook her head in despair.

He patted the seat beside the driver's seat. "Get in. I'll leave you at the Thornes'."

She hesitated. He reached out, and she took his hand, climbing in beside him. He grinned again, gunned the engine, and brought the jeep around in a sharp U turn. He spoke in a loud voice, above the sound of the engine. "Now I want you to do me a favor. Just a little one. It won't hurt a living soul. There's a road up ahead that leads to a knoll. I've been there for picnics once or twice. Let me take you there."

She turned her head away.

His temper rose. "I just want to talk to you for five or ten minutes. For God's sake, Cindy."

She said in a barely audible voice, "Please, Mark. I don't want to talk."

"Maybe you want what I want."

The jeep picked up speed, rocking as it had on

A Quiet Place

the night of the picnic. She covered her eyes with the palms of her hands. She said, "Stop it, Mark. You'll kill us both." She took her hands away from her eyes. The side road loomed dead ahead. The jeep was angling across the blacktop, going toward the turnoff at a fancy clip. Mark leaned out, his right hand high on the steering wheel, his face impassive. The jeep was going straight toward a stand of pine, tires screeching. Mark's hand pulled at the wheel as he tried to make the turn. Cindy half rose in her seat. A stump lay directly ahead, a big one, two or three feet high. She jumped. As the jeep hit the stump, it jerked sharply to the left.

She lay still on a bed of moss. Her breath came in short gasps. She sat up slowly, clutching at her right arm, looking down at her right hand, flexing the fingers. She turned her head slowly, facing the jeep. She saw the top of Mark's head. He was lying across both front seats, perfectly still, dappled sunlight all around. One leg was bent at the knee, resting against the steering column, keeping him from sliding to the ground.

A bird fluttered in a nearby tree, fussing and calling. The bird was silent. A bee hummed softly a few

A Quiet Place

feet away, sunlight glinting on its wings. Mark's hair stirred in a soft breeze. Cindy screamed. The sound hung in the quiet air. She rose, trembling, and moved toward the jeep. She put her hand out and, moaning softly, touched Mark's forehead. She shut her eyes and her head bobbed gently in a gesture of thanks. "Oh, God," she said.

She walked around behind the jeep. It was tilted at a sharp angle, about to topple. She fell to her knees and started sobbing. "Oh, God. Please," she wailed. She half crawled toward the blacktop, watching the jeep, rising to her feet again. She gave the jeep a long look, then stared wildly up and down the road. She started toward the Sears' house. She whispered, "Help. Someone, help."

She straightened up, standing still, looking toward Finger Point, listening. It was just a distant hum at first; then it came louder. As the truck came around the bend, going slowly, at a steady pace, Cindy whispered, "Don't shake the earth." She gestured to make Ike stop in the road, keeping him from coming close.

He climbed down from the cab and stood looking at the jeep. "My God," he said under his breath. He turned to Cindy. "Stay where you are."

A Quiet Place

He turned deliberately, going back to the cab of the truck, leaning in, flicking a switch, starting the emergency blinkers going. He walked around to the back of the truck and came back with a coil of rope. He said, "Come along with me. Keep clear of the jeep."

He stood on the high side of the stump, studying the jeep again. He said, "You stay here."

He walked back around the jeep and looped the rope around the steering column, tying a knot. He threw the coil of rope across Mark's body, toward Cindy. She reached down and picked it up, holding it loosely until Ike came around and took it. "Move back," he said. "Toward those trees."

Cindy did as she was told. He moved back slowly, watching the jeep, keeping the rope taut, his big hands working back, one after the other, toward the trees. He said tensely, "Can you tie a bowline?"

"I think so," she said.

"Thinking isn't good enough. Tell you what you do. Take the end of the rope. Keep it pulled as tight as you can." He jerked his head back toward the nearest tree. "Wrap it around the trunk of that tree. Take it two or three times around. Make it cross over itself."

A Quiet Place

"I'll make a half hitch."

"A half hitch will do nicely."

Ike came back and took a few more turns around the tree. When the rope was secure, they moved down to the jeep. "Better not move him," Ike said. He reached across Mark's right shoulder, pulling his shirt up, pressing gently against Mark's stomach, under his ribs. "Still has a heartbeat," Ike said. "Took a nasty blow on the head."

They walked around to the low side again. Mark's knee, the one that rested against the dashboard, was covered with blood. His forehead had turned yellow, swelling just below the hairline. His eyes were shut, almost squinting. Ike said, "You stay with him."

Cindy said, pressing hard, "Go now. Go call a doctor, Ike."

Ike said, "If he comes to, don't let him move. Come to think of it, I better stay. It's better if you go back to Mia's. Go now. I'll stand watch. If he tries to get up, he'll hurt himself worse. This thing is sitting at a terrible angle."

Cindy nodded and started back along the road, walking fast, stumbling. As she turned into the

A Quiet Place

Sears' driveway, she called out, "Mia. Where are you?"

The place was quiet. She struggled on. A screen door opened, and Stevie came out. The door banged shut. He moved toward the band. Cindy said, "Stevie, where's your mother?"

Stevie kept going. Cindy said hotly. "I spoke to you, Stevie. Where's your mother?"

The child stopped. He turned and regarded her silently, then kept moving toward the barn.

Mia came to the door. She said, "Cindy. What happened? What's the matter?"

"Call an ambulance right away. There's been an accident down the road." She gestured toward the place where Ike was waiting.

Mia said, "What kind of accident? Where did it happen?"

"Call an ambulance," she repeated weakly. "Tell them to come along this road."

Mia disappeared behind the screen door, into the shadows. Cindy moved slowly toward the house, through the yellow grass, up the gentle slope.

Cindy's eyelids fluttered. The room was dim. Mia was sitting in a straight-backed chair, beside the couch where Cindy lay. Cindy said, "What's that funny taste in my mouth?"

"It must be the brandy. I gave you some brandy."

"What time is it?"

"Seven thirty. I'll take you back to the Thornes' soon."

Cindy turned her head away. She shut her eyes and drew a quick breath. She said, "Is he dead?"

"The man in the jeep? Not as far as I know. He was conscious when the ambulance picked him up."

"How do you know?"

"I talked to Ike's mother. Ike went back to his barn to pick up tackle. He thought he better pull the jeep off the stump. He said it was a hazard the way it was."

Cindy drew a convulsive breath. She wept quietly, dabbing at her eyes with the back of her hand. Mia got up and went to the kitchen. She brought back a box of paper handkerchiefs. Cindy said, "Thank you, Mia." She shook her head. "What a mess! How did Ike sound when you talked to him?"

Mia gave her a searching look. "I didn't talk to Ike. I talked to his mother."

"That's right. You told me you talked to his mother."

A Quiet Place

"There's a nasty bruise on your right cheek."

"Didn't Ike tell his mother who was in the jeep?"

"Was it someone he knew?"

"It was Mark Duncan."

Mia's eyes widened. She said, reflectively, "I saw Mark Duncan just yesterday. Down in the village. He asked about you."

She shut her eyes.

"Were you in the jeep when it hit that stump?"

Cindy nodded. "I suppose most people think he's bad news. And he's older than I am. I suppose he's had several dozen girls."

Mia poured Cindy a finger of brandy. Cindy made a face. "No, thanks," she said.

Mia said, "I suppose Mark Duncan is fascinating." She put the glass of brandy on a table.

"I understand Mark. I think he understands me. That's important, isn't it?"

"It certainly is."

"But he is bad news. I see that, too. I guess I knew it when I first met him." She sat up slowly. She said, "I want to go back to the Thornes' now."

12

Mia parked the car near a concrete ramp. At the top of the ramp was a sign. EMERGENCY ONLY.

They walked across to the visitors' entrance. As they moved through the doors, Mia said, "I remember now."

"Remember what?"

"The hospital smell." She whispered, sounding like a scheming child, "I don't like the smell at all."

The woman at the desk was plump. Her face was like a fortress under siege. Cindy said, "I came to visit Mr. Duncan. Can you tell me what floor he's on, please?"

A Quiet Place

The woman flipped through a rotary file. She said, "How old were you on your last birthday?"

"I was seventeen."

"Minors aren't allowed in ICU."

"But he's a friend of mine. He wants to see me."

"We have to abide by hospital rules."

Mia said, "I'll visit him then. What floor's he on?"

The woman eyed her suspiciously. "The intensive care unit is on the second floor."

Mia said firmly, "Cindy, wait for me in the car."

Cindy went out. She stood in the shadow of Mia's car, looking up at the building. She sat down on a concrete wall. Three people drove up in a gleaming car and parked, two men and a woman, all middle-aged. They got out of the car and banged the doors shut, one, two, three. In flat, slightly nasal tones, one of the women said, "I can't believe it. I really can't."

The other woman said, "No. Neither can I."

All three moved toward the visitors' entrance. As the man pulled the glass door open, it flashed the sun's reflection into Cindy's eyes. She heard Mia calling her name. When she turned, Mia was standing outside the emergency entrance, beckoning wildly. Cindy slid off the wall and moved up the ramp. "Look natural," Mia said.

Cindy laughed. "I'll go along with you."

"Old fussbudget," Mia said.

"Hope she didn't see me go up the ramp."

"Didn't you see?" Mia said impishly. "I waited until those people went in. The old sourpuss is busy by now, telling them the hospital rules."

They moved through a corridor that led to another and went up a short flight of stairs. Mia said, "Notice which way you came. Remember how to get out of here."

In the second-floor corridor, Mia said, "Now you wait here."

Cindy stood smiling, watching Mia approach an orderly. A nurse came by. The nurse asked, "May I help you, dear?"

Cindy said, "No, thanks. I'm waiting for someone."

Mia came back. She pointed to a door. She said, "I'll wait in the car."

Cindy hesitated outside the door. She heard the springs of a bed creaking. She went in. There were four beds in the room, two of them empty. Mark lay in a bed by the window. Another man lay on a

A Quiet Place

bed in a corner. Mark was leaning against his pillows. His head was bandaged. His face was drawn. Cindy said, "Hello."

He said, "It's good to see you." One of his arms rested on his stomach. His chest, where it showed above the sheet, was taped all the way around. "It was nice of you to come."

"I wanted to, of course. I was sorry not to call. But I didn't want to call from the Thornes'."

"It doesn't matter. I don't like to talk on the telephone."

"When will they let you out of here?"

"In a week or so."

She moved closer and sat in a chair. The bed was high. Mark looked down. He reached up and pushed aside a strand of his hair where it hung out over the bandage. "What have you been doing?"

"I've been leading the simple life. Up early and to bed at nine." She looked toward the opposite corner of the room. The other occupant was dozing. She watched Mark's face. She said, "You're a son of a bitch, you know."

"The little lady's tongue is sharp."

"You could have killed us both."

A Quiet Place

He flushed. His mouth became a thin line. Then he shrugged and said, "I like your prickly side."

Her lip quivered. "You're too damned cool for your own good."

"If you came to insult me, shove off."

A tear ran down her cheek. He reached out and took her hand. She said, "I didn't mean to lose my temper. I came to make peace. I couldn't help it. When I saw your face, I couldn't help it."

"Let's talk. I'd like to talk to you awhile."

"That's right. I forgot. You wanted to talk. That's why you were taking me up that hill."

He watched her coldly.

She said, "I'll stop. I'm sorry. I'll stop." She was silent, looking at the bedframe, at a crank that adjusted it to suit the patient. She said, "Why did you come looking for me?"

"I came on the chance that I'd find you alone."

"There was very little chance of that." Then she asked, "Why were you so frantic when you finally found me?"

"It started when the Thornes said you'd gone off with Ike. There they were, the two of them, rocking on their porch."

She tapped the plaster cast that covered one of

A Quiet Place

his legs. It made a hollow sound. She asked, "Why are you in the intensive care unit?"

"They put me here because my head was bruised. They thought there was a chance my brain had been damaged. They're moving me out of here tomorrow." He squinted as he turned his eyes to the window. He asked abruptly, "Do you love Ike Thorne?"

His arm lay against the sheet, dark hair against tan skin. She answered slowly. "Love is a very important word."

He said, "Go on."

She shook her head. "I don't want to talk about it now." She stood up and looked toward the window. She said, "I came here with Mia Sears. You know Ben and Mia Sears."

He nodded. "I don't know Ben. I've talked to Mia a few times. Mia's a funny mouse of a woman."

"She's not really a mouse at all. She's quiet, but she has backbone," Cindy said. "Are you sure your brain wasn't damaged?"

"Do you think it was?"

She smiled. "Maybe a little."

"My comb is on the shelf in the bathroom. Get it for me, will you, Cindy?"

A Quiet Place

She gave him the comb. "Watch the bandage when you comb your hair." She went back to the window and looked down. Mia was sitting in her car. Cindy said, "I better go. I wasn't supposed to see you at all. Minors aren't allowed in the intensive care unit. And Mia's waiting."

He said, "Don't go."

"I better, really." She moved over and stood by the bed. "Remember to write."

"I will. But stay awhile. We've left so much unsaid."

"There's nothing more to talk about."

"Sit down a minute more. Mia will wait. When are you leaving for New York?"

"I'm leaving tomorrow afternoon." She leaned against a corner of the mattress, looking at the tops of the trees outside. A cardinal flew up from among the leaves, a flash of vermillion against the green. Someone bustled along the hall. A light knock sounded on the half-closed door. "Come in," Mark said.

A nurse poked her head in. She smiled pleasantly at Cindy, then at Mark. "A visitor," she said. "That's nice." She glanced at Mark's roommate and disappeared.

A Quiet Place

Cindy said, "I'm going now."

Mark nodded. "My mother and Sam will be here soon."

"Where's your father?"

"He's coming from Boston this afternoon. He didn't hear the news until this morning. He'd been out with what he calls the boys. He chewed me out for wrecking the jeep. My father's a jerk. He's a—"

"Stop it, Mark." She blew her nose on a paper handkerchief, wadded the handkerchief, holding it tight in one of her hands.

He said, "Trash basket's on the other side."

She walked around the bed and aimed at the basket. The missile hit its mark with a satisfying sound. She said, "Goodbye. Take care."

13

Mrs. Thorne and Cindy cleared the table, stacked the dishes in the washer. Television sounded in the living room. Mrs. Thorne touched Cindy's arm. "You promised you'd play your guitar for us."

Cindy glanced toward the door, hesitating. Mrs. Thorne said, "They're watching the news. After that you can play for us."

Cindy said, "Could we close the door a minute?"

Mrs. Thorne gave her a frightened look, dried her hands and closed the door.

Cindy said abruptly, "I love you, you know. I love you all."

Mrs. Thorne's hand went up, reaching out. Cindy

A Quiet Place

gave her a hug, kissing her cheek, then stood back. "I think I better leave on Monday. Mia's going back with me." Cindy looked away, suddenly tense. "She knows a lot about art, you know, about painting and sculpture and things like that. She's been wanting to visit some art museums."

"We have a fine museum here."

"It is, indeed, a fine museum. But she wants to take a trip. She needs a change."

Mrs. Thorne's eyes were a clear blue. Her face was almost beautiful. She said, "Poor Mia. I guess she should have stayed in Boston."

The door swung open and Ike came in, shaking his head and grinning to himself. "Father's cussin' the unions again." He turned to Cindy, making a face of mock despair. "I told him unions are here to stay. Tell him they're here to stay, Cindy."

She looked up, brightening.

"Go on in and tell him, Cindy."

Mrs. Thorne said, "Please, Ike. Don't be silly."

"What's the matter, Mother? What's the trouble?"

Mrs. Thorne said, "Ask your father to turn the television off. Cindy said she'll sing us a few songs."

A Quiet Place

Ike said, "It's chily tonight. I can feel fall in the air."

Mrs. Thorne said, "I hate the thought of winter."

"It's chilly enough for a fire right now. I'll light a fire in the living-room stove. Take off the dampness and give us some cheer."

Cindy went up and brought down her guitar. Ike lit the fire and set the damper. He settled down in a dark corner. His father said, "I had a girl back in high school. She played the guitar like a perfect angel."

Mrs. Thorne said, "Angels play harps."

"Don't be so literal-minded."

Cindy sat cross-legged on the floor.

Ike said, "They both make music."

Mr. Thorne said, "My, but that girl was pretty."

His wife said, "Her name was Rosie Hartell. Rosie got prettier every year. Nobody's seen her since she went off to college."

Cindy started tuning her guitar, plucking one string at a time.

Mrs. Thorne sat close to her husband. He took her hand. "Nobody ever was as pretty as you. Excepting maybe Cindy here. It's just that I like to remember sometimes."

A Quiet Place

"I know it, dear. Everybody likes to remember."

Cindy struck a chord. She said, "My sister taught me to play." Her voice was very clear. The first was a song about unrequited love. When she finished singing it, she said, "I'm rusty."

Mrs. Thorne said, "It was lovely, dear."

Cindy sang half a dozen songs. She said, "Here's one my father taught me." She sang in a faintly plaintive voice:

> Hush, little baby, don't say a word.
> Papa's gonna buy you a mockin'bird.
> And if that mockin'bird don't sing,
> Papa's gonna buy you a diamond ring.

She sang half a dozen more couplets. As she sang the last one, her voice was soft. She measured her words.

> And if that horse and cart fall down,
> You'll still be the sweetest li'l baby in town.

One of the logs cracked loudly. The fire hissed. Cindy said, "That's my favorite lullaby."

A Quiet Place

Mrs. Thorne said, "I didn't know your father sang."

"He doesn't sing much, but he likes to sing."

Ike leaned forward into the light. He said, "Sing the first one again. About Barbara Allen."

Mrs. Thorne said, "Maybe she doesn't want to, Ike."

Cindy stretched. She got up slowly.

Ike clapped a hand over one of his knees. He said, "I think I forgot to light the hen pen. Come out and keep me company."

Cindy said, "I'm sleepy. I think I'll take a bath."

Ike said, "The fresh air will bring you around. You can take a bath later."

Cindy put her guitar away, closing the case and flipping the catches. She followed Ike into the kitchen, took a sweater off one of the chairs. She put it on. He held the outside door open. He said, "You're as bad as Clover. You hate to come in when you're outside, and you hate to go outside when you're in." He made a happy sound in his throat. "Come to think of it, it's good to be like that. It's a sign you like to be where you are."

They went to the hen house. As he opened the

A Quiet Place

door, he said, "Can't think why I forgot the light." He flipped the switch.

"It's not like you forgetting things."

"Let's go have a look at the sow."

"I hope the little ones come before I leave."

"I hate to think about you leaving."

"I always feel sad at the end of summer. So does my father. All the summer people do, I guess."

"Some of us feel sad too. Old Henry talks nonsense about summer people. But even Old Henry doesn't mean what he says. He likes a lot of the summer people. And he hates to see winter coming on."

The moon was rising above the bay, nearly full, standing in a light mist. The waters were still, reflecting the moon as it was in the sky. Ike stopped, leaning against the truck. "Pretty soon most of the cottages hereabouts will be boarded up against the winter weather. My egg route will dwindle. Winter is bleak in a place like this. In years past I didn't mind." He gestured toward the barn, toward the place where the tie room was. "I have a little radio in there. I keep it up on one of the beams. Last winter after Father's accident, I played it when I

A Quiet Place

was milking. It was company enough with the animals there. And Father's accident was in later winter. It seemed that spring was already starting."

"It was," she said.

"What do you mean, Cindy?"

"I meant that spring starts before we see it. It starts under the ground. Things start to grow long before we see them." Cindy raised one of her feet and tugged at the strap of one of her sandals.

Ike's voice was very soft, almost a whisper. "Now I'm like my mother and father. I hate to think of winter. If only. . . . His chin was up. He was looking toward the bay again. He went on, in the same soft voice, "But sometimes winter is a grand time here. I like it at sunrise when the snow has drifted. Right here, when I cross to the barn, the shadows of the pines lie across my path." He watched her face. "If I could only be sure I'd see you again."

"Of course you will. But you do see that I can't promise things. I'm much too young." She stood straight. "And the world's so big."

He looked away. She said, "What is it, Ike?"

"When I sent you off to Mia's for the ambulance, I didn't know you'd been in the jeep when it hit that stump. I didn't know you'd been with Mark Duncan."

"I know it, Ike. I'm sorry. I should have told you. I don't suppose you even knew I knew him."

"I knew you knew him. Saw his jeep in front of your house. Late one night." His voice was low. "Cindy, there's something I want to ask you."

"I guess you have a right to ask."

"Where was he taking you?"

"Up that road. To a picnic ground."

"Mother said he stopped here to give you a sweater. When she said you were at Mia's, he kept the sweater. He said he thought it was yours, but he wasn't sure."

"The sweater wasn't mine. He knew it wasn't mine."

"What would you have done if he hadn't hit the stump? What would have happened at the picnic ground?"

"You're right of course." She ran her hand impatiently through her hair. "I suppose we would have made love. I don't know. I really don't know."

He shut his eyes, turning away. A whippoorwill called across the road, back in the lot where they'd

A Quiet Place

taken the oxen to bring in the logs. Ike's hands bunched into fists.

Cindy said, "Ike, for God's sake."

His voice was hoarse. "I want you to promise. Promise me, Cindy."

"I just can't promise things, Ike."

"I mean promise I'll see you again. That's all. Just promise that."

"Of course, Ike. Of course you will."

His hands relaxed at his sides. He pushed himself away from the truck and moved toward the barn. The barn was dark. Ike walked in, around the tractor, moving easily in the dark. The light went on in front of the sow's stall. Cindy moved over and looked in. The animal lay on her side, breathing hard. Her pink belly budged outward, covered with spots and coarse hair. Her teats were full, ready for nursing. Cindy smiled gently. Ike stirred, close to her elbow. He said softly, "You love it here, don't you, Cindy?"

"I love the animals and the smells. I love you all." Suddenly she said, "I've decided I better leave on Monday. Mia's going with me. She wants to go to some art museums. I'll show her around. It will do her good."

A Quiet Place

Ike faced her, his eyes clear. He smiled. "It will," he said. "I like to think of you showing Mia the sights."

Cindy said, "Mia's feeling guilty about leaving Ben."

"I'll look in on him. And Mother will too. Mother likes to brood."

"She doesn't seem to me like the brooding type."

"She likes helpless things. She likes taking care of people. Mother has a strong maternal streak."

Cindy looked up at Ike. "Well, her son's not helpless. Not in the least."

The room Cindy slept in faced the bay. Her window was open at the top. She leaned against the window frame; her hair stirred slightly in the night air. The barn and the yard were dark, the weather vane etched against the night sky. The moon was still high, shining brightly, behind the branches of a tall pine. Cindy studied the yard, the familiar shapes, changed by the depth of the night shadows.

Her face was impassive. She stood, unmoving for a long time, watching silently, then turned away. She went to her suitcase. She opened it and rummaged in a side pocket, taking out the mouse that

A Quiet Place

wore the flowered dress and lace-fringed apron. She put it on the table beside her bed, turned back the covers, switched off the light, and slipped into bed. She lay in the dark, looking up at the sky.

14

The day was bright and chilly. Ike was wearing a leather jacket. He stood by the old sedan, his arm draped over the door. Mr. Thorne was on the porch, waving. He called, "Come back soon. Winter's hard, but it's lovely here. We'll welcome you any time of year."

Mrs. Thorne stood by Cindy. "He means it, you know. Come back just as soon as you can."

Cindy said, "I'll miss you." She gave Mrs. Thorne a longing look, put her arms around her and kissed her on the cheek. Mrs. Thorne said, "You take care of yourself, dear. And keep Mia out of trouble. See that she comes back safe and sound."

A Quiet Place

Mia stood by the mailbox at the end of her drive, wearing quiet city clothes. "The children know I'm going," she said. "But I don't want a lot of tearful good-byes."

Ike climbed out of the driver's seat and held the rear door open for Mia. He handed in her bag and closed the door. As Ike turned the car around, Cindy caught a glimpse of Jenny and Stevie, running toward the house. They stopped when they saw the car, waved to Ike, and disappeared. "They didn't see me," Mia said.

As the car rolled down a long hill, where the turnpike stretched into the distance, where pines towered high on either side, Mia said, "It's exciting. I've only flown three times before."

The car hummed along the road. Traffic was light. A Volkswagen bus overtook them. On its roof a ragged canvas flapped wildly in the wind. Its driver had long, dark hair. Ike said, "Where did you fly to when you flew before?"

"First I flew to Boston from New York." When she spoke again, her voice was light, her eyes shining. "And I flew again when Ben and I went to France."

They stopped at a tollgate, Ike took a ticket, and

A Quiet Place

they drove on. Ike said, "I never knew you and Ben had been to France. Did you go on your honeymoon?"

"We'd been married six months. An uncle left Ben two thousand dollars. We hadn't expected it. So off we went. We went to Paris first and then down to the Alpes Maritimes. France is lovely. Ben and I stayed in a storybook town."

Cindy said, "I've always wanted to go to France."

Ike swung off the turnpike at a place where the land was flat. Factories and supermarkets lined the road. Cindy looked at her watch. Jet engines screamed overhead. The car trembled as the plane moved off. The road was smooth. Ike drove slowly, eyes front. The flat surface of the field stretched into the distance. Without warning, a small twin-engine plane flew in beside them, passing them at more than twice their speed, touching down, taxiing along the runway, obscured for a moment by a structure holding lights and signals, appearing again, slowing down.

Mia said, "No need to park in the parking lot. There's a place in front of the terminal building."

Ike parked and walked around, taking the bags

A Quiet Place

and Cindy's guitar. Cindy said, "Let me take the guitar."

The terminal was concrete and tinted glass. An electric eye activated the doors. Cindy said, "We may as well check our bags through. No sense carrying all this on."

Ike stood with them as they waited at the counter. Most of the people were wearing city clothes, a few flamboyant summer clothes, bright slacks, red and yellow shirts. Five teen-agers lounged close by, two girls and three boys, all wearing jeans. The girls wore sandals, and the boys wore heavy workingmen's shoes. One of the boys nodded to Cindy, and Cindy nodded solemnly back. Ike was absorbed in thoughts of his own. When they had their tickets, Mia said, "Excuse me a minute."

Cindy said, "We'll meet you in the downstairs lounge."

Ike and Cindy moved down the steps. They sat on a sofa covered in plastic. Ike pushed the button on an ashtray beside the couch. He said, "Look at this. Quite a gadget." Cindy smiled at him, a little stiffly. He said, "My, but you're quiet."

"I don't feel like talking, that's all."

A Quiet Place

He said sadly, "I'm a fish out of water in a place like this."

"Everyone feels that way sometimes."

Ike smiled for the first time since breakfast. "I suppose they do. You're right, of course."

Mia came down the stairs. Cindy said, "Mia looks fine in her city clothes."

"Doesn't look natural to me at all." As Cindy got up, he said, "Do you wear city clothes?"

"Not very often. I'm happier in dungarees."

A big yellow and white plane came in and taxied close to the terminal building. The speaker tweeted and squawked. A metallic voice announced their flight. Ike stood by, unbuttoning his jacket. He said, "I think I'll say good-bye to you now."

Cindy looked up at him. His eyes were clear, his voice steady. He said, "Cindy, I'll be seeing you soon. All of us want you to come back. Father and Mother and Mia and me. We all want you back." He looked away, taking a handkerchief out of his pocket and blotting his forehead.

Mia said, "Good-bye, Ike. If I call, will you meet me when I come back?"

His face broke into a broad grin. "You just call

A Quiet Place

and don't forget." He gestured toward a restaurant. "I'll buy you supper here at the airport. Or lunch. Or whatever. You can tell me all about New York."

Cindy and Mia found a seat together. Cindy took off her raincoat. She folded it. She felt a lump in one of its pockets. She was puzzled by it until she reached in and took out her mouse. She held it up for Mia to see. She said, "I almost left Mouse behind this morning. I was leaving the guest room when I saw her on the table by the bed."

She tossed her raincoat onto the rack. "Here, Mia. Sit by the window."

"I'll sit here until after we take off. I'm always frightened when the plane is taking off."

They settled down. Mia admired the mouse. She said, "Her clothes bear the marks of loving care. And of long winter evenings."

Cindy nodded. "My father gave her to me. When I was little, my father called me Mouse." She leaned her head against the window glass.

A latecomer, a man in a dark suit, carrying a small bag, was running across the sunlit apron toward the plane. The voice of the hostess, light and cheerful, rose above the muffled sounds in the cabin. "Good afternoon. You just made it."

A Quiet Place

People stood along the low fence in front of the terminal building, some of them waving. Others had gathered on a second-floor balcony to watch the departing plane. A little boy in a bright-red shirt strained to climb to the top of the railing. His mother jerked him back and took his hand. The ends of the balcony were deserted. The people in the building, behind the tinted glass, were ghostly, monochromatic shapes.

The seat belt sign went on. The hostess walked along the aisle, smiling and looking down at the laps of the passengers. The engine whined and roared.

Ike moved up to the fence at a corner of the building, far from the other well-wishers. Cindy's hand went up. She waved wildly. He stood as before, watching the plane, the sun in his eyes.

Cindy watched as the plane taxied to the end of the runway, an expanse of brown grass all around, sheds and houses in the distance.

As the plane gathered speed, Mia took hold of one of Cindy's wrists. Cindy put a hand over Mia's hand. She said, "You really are afraid."

Mia's hand tightened on Cindy's wrist. The runway flashed by in a blur of concrete. The plane lifted, tilting upward, engines screaming. Mia relaxed her grip. She said, "What happened to the mouse?"

Cindy clutched at her lap. She leaned over, running her hand across the carpet at her feet. She smiled as she retrieved the mouse. "Will you keep her for me?"

Mia laughed, turning the mouse in her hand, tucking it carefully into her handbag. Cindy rested her head against the window glass again. The plane was circling, banking and climbing. She caught sight of the airport, the terminal building, part of the field, two cars moving on a narrow gray strip. She turned to Mia. Her voice barely rose above the sound of the engines. "Are there men who are both exciting and good?"

"I suppose there are," Mia said.

"I've never known anyone as good as Ike."

The plane climbed steadily, flying above a pine-covered island. A fragment of a white roof caught the sun and disappeared behind a cluster of trees.

The air was clear, the water shallow green at first, cold blue where it grew deep. Far below, she saw a

A Quiet Place

ketch on a broad reach, heading south, her sails gleaming in the afternoon sun. The wing of the plane, glaring, misting at its tip, slid across the sailboat, leaving an expanse of sea, broken now and then by a fleck of white.

ABOUT THE AUTHOR

Peter Burchard was born in Washington, D.C., went to school in New Jersey and Connecticut, and was graduated from the Philadelphia Museum School of Art.

During World War II he was on convoy duty in the North Atlantic and his drawings appeared in *Yank* magazine. In 1948 he became a free-lance designer and illustrator. He is the author of ten books, among them *Bimby, Jed, Rat Hell,* and *North by Night*. His work has been highly praised; the New York *Times* describes him as having a "splendid facility for characterization."

His stories and reviews have appeared in national

A Quiet Place

magazines. He was a Guggenheim Fellow in 1966 and recently received a Christopher Award.

Mr. Burchard lives in New York City and Stonington, Connecticut. He and his wife sail a boat of their own, have lived and traveled in Europe and spent a number of summers in Maine. Mr. Burchard is the father of three, two daughters and a son.